The Lost World

MICHAEL CRICHTON

Level 4

Retold by Janet McAlpin
Series Editors: Andy Hopkins and Jocelyn Potter

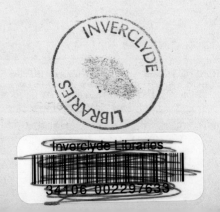

Pearson Education Limited
Edinburgh Gate, Harlow,
Essex CM20 2JE, England
and Associated Companies throughout the world.

ISBN 0 582 41694 9

First published by Arrow Books 1997
© Michael Crichton 1995
This adaptation first published by Penguin Books 1997
Published by Addison Wesley Longman Limited and Penguin Books Ltd. 1998
This edition first published 1999

Third impression 2001

Text copyright © Janet McAlpin 1997
Cover artwork copyright © 1997 by MCA Publishing Rights,
a division of Universal Studios, Inc.
Illustrations copyright © Chris Chaisty 1997
All rights reserved

The moral right of the adapter and of the illustrator has been asserted

Typeset by Rowland Phototypesetting Limited, Bury St Edmunds, Suffolk
Set in 11/13pt Monotype Bembo
Printed in Spain by Mateu Cromo, S.A. Pinto (Madrid)

Published by Pearson Education Limited in association with
Penguin Books Ltd., both companies being subsidiaries of Pearson Plc

For a complete list of the titles available in the Penguin Readers series please write to your local
Pearson Education office or to: Marketing Department, Penguin Longman Publishing,
Penguin Books Ltd, 5 Bentinck Street, London W1M 5RN.

Contents

Introduction

"Suppose — just suppose — that we hear of more animals there," Levine said. "Would you help with my expedition?"

Malcolm finished his beer and pushed the bottle to one side. He stared at Levine. "Yes," he said finally.

It is six years since the secret disaster at Jurassic Park. The dinosaurs were destroyed and the Park was closed. But now people are finding dead animals again – are they dinosaurs?

Something is still alive . . .

Michael Crichton was born in Chicago in 1942. He went to Harvard College and Harvard Medical School, and taught at Cambridge University when he was twenty-three years old. While he was studying to be a doctor, he also wrote books. One of his early books was *The Andromeda Strain*, a science-fiction story which was made into a highly successful movie.

Crichton decided that he was "too imaginative" to be a doctor, and he gave up the medical profession in order to write full-time. Since then he has written over fifteen books, including *Disclosure*, *Jurassic Park* and *Airframe*. He wrote *The Lost World*, which continues the story of *Jurassic Park*, in 1995. His stories are usually about new scientific ideas that are dangerous and that seem frighteningly possible. Crichton has written and directed successful movies, like *Coma* (1978). He also made the famous TV program *ER*, about a hospital in Chicago. He lives and works in Los Angeles.

The movie *Jurassic Park* (1993) was made by Steven Spielberg. It was one of the most successful movies ever made. Spielberg made *The Lost World* in 1998, with Jeff Goldblum as Dr Ian Malcolm.

Chapter 1   Are Dinosaurs Really Extinct?

"Animals become extinct," said Dr. Ian Malcolm, "Scientists have known this fact for over two hundred years, but the subject didn't really interest us until twenty years ago."

It was August, 1993, and Dr. Malcolm was speaking to a group of scientists. He was dressed all in black, and his tall, thin body was bent over a walking stick.

"In the 1970s," he continued, "people began to see how changes to the planet were causing animal species to die out. Could the same thing happen to humans one day? Nobody was sure. We began to ask how species can become extinct.

"For example," he said, "the dinosaurs died out about sixty-five million years ago, but did they die out slowly or suddenly? In 1980, a new discovery suggested that it happened suddenly, after a giant meteorite hit the earth. This theory seemed exciting. But it's wrong. The fact is that extinction is happening all the time."

Dr. Malcolm paused, and then gave some figures. "We guess that there have been fifty billion species on this planet since life began. Today there are fifty million. That means that for every species that exists today, one thousand have become extinct. It seems to take about four million years for most species, one million for mammals. Why does extinction happen in this regular way?

"One answer is that our planet is always changing. Ice comes and goes, forests die and grow, and animals change too. The dinosaurs could change, so why didn't they?

"I suggest that it is behavior, not change, that explains extinction, and we can look to the latest thinking in Chaos Theory to help us understand how this happens."

He looked around the room. "We all know the idea of

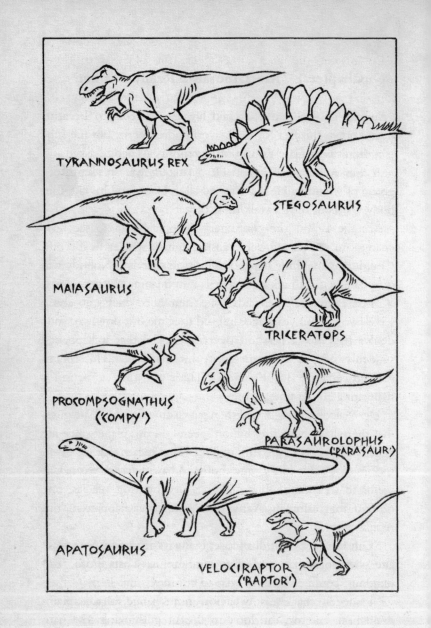

TYRANNOSAURUS REX

STEGOSAURUS

MAIASAURUS

TRICERATOPS

PROCOMPSOGNATHUS
('COMPY')

PARASAUROLOPHUS
('PARASAUR')

APATOSAURUS

VELOCIRAPTOR
('RAPTOR')

the edge of chaos," he said, and many heads nodded. "We imagine this as a place where the old and the new are always at war. Animal species seem to exist on this edge. On one side is too much change, and on the other is too little change. To move away from the edge is to become extinct."

A hand went up. "You had a question?" Malcolm asked.

A thin young man in his early thirties stood. "It's an interesting idea," he said, "but not easy to test. Bones don't tell us about behavior, computers can't help much, and we can't test extinction theories on living things."

"Yes," said Malcolm shortly, "but what's your point?"

"Just this," said the young man. "If extinction was the result of behavior, did all dinosaurs change their behavior everywhere at the same time? Not likely. So there could be some left, somewhere on earth. Couldn't you look for them?"

"You're talking about a Lost World," Malcolm said.

"I'm talking about some real corner of the planet," said the young man.

"Impossible," said Malcolm coldly and continued his talk.

◆

Shortly after noon, Malcolm stepped into the hot sunshine with a woman. They made a strange pair. At forty, Malcolm looked bent and tired. His younger friend was strong and healthy. She was Sarah Harding, a scientist famous for her special studies of African animals.

Sarah Harding was still at college when they met. Some years later, Malcolm had a serious accident in Costa Rica, and Harding spent a long time helping to nurse him. Perhaps they were once lovers. But now they were just good friends.

"What's the story on the 'Lost World' guy?" said Malcolm.

Harding laughed. "Richard Levine? He's rich and selfish, but he's a great scientist. He studies extinct animals."

3

As they spoke, Richard Levine hurried towards them.

"Ah, hell!" Malcolm said.

"Dr. Malcolm," Levine said, coming up. "I was surprised you didn't take my idea more seriously."

"How could I?" Malcolm said. "It's foolish."

"No," said Levine. "It's very possible that dinosaurs still exist. You must know there are reports from the Congo about large animals in the forest, and from Irian Jaya —"

"Any photographs?" asked Malcolm. "No! Just stories."

"Then what about rumors of dead animals in Costa Rica?" said Levine. "I keep getting calls about them."

Malcolm paused. "Recently?"

"The last call was nine months ago," Levine said. "I couldn't get there in time. It was something very large, found dead in the forest."

"And? What happened to it?"

"Burned," said Levine, sadly.

"So nothing is left? Then it's just a story too."

"Perhaps," said Levine. "But I want to know more, and I'm planning to take an expedition to Costa Rica."

Malcolm stared at him. "An expedition? To find a Lost World? Who is going to pay for it?"

"I am," Levine said. "I don't care what it costs. And I hope you will be interested."

"I'm not interested in dinosaurs," Malcolm said.

"But everyone is interested in dinosaurs."

"Not me." He turned on his stick and started to walk off.

"Well, why did you go to Costa Rica, then?" asked Levine.

◆

"You want to know what I've heard?" Levine said, excitedly. They were sitting at a cafe table, drinking beer.

"I've heard that a couple of years ago, a company called InGen found a way to make dinosaurs from cells taken from dinosaur bones. They put them on an island in Costa Rica, but something went wrong. A lot of people were killed, and all the dinosaurs died. And now nobody will talk about it."

"And you believe that?" Malcolm said.

"Not at first I didn't," Levine said. "But the thing is, I keep hearing it. Is it true?"

"You think it's possible to make a dinosaur from cells?"

"Everyone says it's not," said Levine.

"And they're right," Malcolm said, looking at Harding.

Sarah Harding said nothing, just drank her beer. But she remembered something. Once, in hospital, Malcolm was in pain. In his sleep he turned over and over in his bed, speaking of dinosaurs. Sometimes he called them "*raptors*" and "*compys,*" and he seemed afraid. Later, when he was better, she asked him about it, but he just made a joke.

"So the InGen story is not true?" she heard Levine ask.

"Not true," said Malcolm. But the story *was* true.

The company called International Genetics, or InGen, had sent him to an island in Costa Rica in 1989. There was a disaster, and everyone moved quickly to kill the story. Scientists were paid a lot of money to keep silent. For example, InGen paid Malcolm's medical bills for two years.

As time passed, people lost interest in the story. The island was destroyed and the company closed down.

"Suppose – just suppose – that we hear of more animals there," Levine said. "Would you help with my expedition?"

Malcolm finished his beer and pushed the bottle to one side. He stared at Levine. "Yes," he said finally.

Chapter 2   Lizard as Big as a Cow

Harding returned to Africa, and eighteen months passed. Levine continued to plan his expedition. He needed very special equipment, which he ordered from a small company called Thorne Field Systems.

"Everything must be very strong, and very light," Levine told Thorne.

"Impossible," Thorne said, shaking his head. But Doc Thorne was famous for solving problems like this.

Levine was busy traveling. When the next call came from Costa Rica, he returned immediately to meet his contact in San José, and they flew south together in a helicopter.

They flew low over the coast, past fishing villages and deep forests, and landed on a clean, white beach. It was empty, except for a single, dark shape. It looked like a big rock. All around it there were the marks of shoes.

"Who's been here, Marty?" Levine asked his friend.

"The Public Health people came out earlier today," said Marty. They wanted to destroy it. I told them you were coming. I don't know how long they'll wait."

"Then we'd better start right now," Levine said, and ran across the beach with his camera. The pilot ran after him.

"No pictures, *señor*," he said, and took the camera.

"Marty," called Levine. "This is crazy. Why no pictures?"

Marty came up and started arguing with the pilot. Levine hurried away to look at the dead animal on the beach.

It was covered with flies and its smell was bad. The size was roughly the same as a cow, but it was not a mammal. The skin was hairless, and the color was once green. Was it a lizard?

Up the beach, Marty was still shouting at the pilot, who kept shaking his head. Levine heard a noise and looked up to see another helicopter arriving – a white one, with red words on the side. Levine turned back to the dead animal.

He saw that the neck was very long, but the head was in the sand. He needed to dig, but first he looked at the back legs. These were very strong, much bigger than the front legs. Could this animal stand on two legs?

Levine hurried away to look at the dead animal on the beach. It was covered with flies and its smell was bad.

Marty came up. "I'm sorry," he said. "I tried my best."

Further up the beach the white helicopter landed. Men in uniforms began getting out.

"Marty. What do you think this animal is?"

"Well I can only guess. It's very large of course, but I think it's a new kind of lizard. It's obviously not from Costa Rica. My guess is it came from the Galapagos, or . . ."

"Marty. It's *not* a lizard. I'll show you. We just need to dig out the head. Give me your knife."

Marty put his knife in Levine's hand. Up the beach, men began shouting and running toward them.

"What are they saying, Marty?" Levine asked.

"They're saying to get back."

"Say we're busy," Levine said, bending over the animal.

But the men kept shouting, and suddenly there was a loud noise. Levine looked up to see they were lighting flame throwers. He ran toward them, shouting "No! No!" But they pushed past him and pointed the flames at the dead animal.

"Stop them, Marty," Levine shouted, but it was too late. They watched as the skin burned black. Suddenly, inside the flames, Levine saw the bones of the long neck and a pointed head with sharp teeth. And then there was nothing but the red flames burning brightly against the evening sky.

♦

Levine sat in the bar of the San José airport, waiting for his plane back to the States. Marty sat with him.

"Marty," Levine said. "What's going on here? That was a very important find on that beach. Why was it destroyed?"

"Well," said Marty, "It's a big problem here. Every so often they find one of these strange dead animals on the coast. It started about five years ago."

"What happens to them?"

"They are always destroyed, just as you saw today.

The government wants to make sure nobody finds out."

"Why?"

"They're worried about health, Richard. Costa Rica has some of the best health care in the world, but now there is a new sickness along the coast. They can't find a cause."

"So they think the sickness comes from the dead animals?"

"Maybe. They can't find out where the animals come from."

"Have they searched?"

"They've sent search parties all over the country."

"What about the islands?" Levine asked.

"Yes, but that's a big job," Marty said. "There are a lot of islands, and some of them are privately owned."

"Which ones?" Levine asked.

"Well, let's see. There's Isla Nublar – an American company called InGen used it for a number of years."

"Was it searched?"

"They flew over it. Nothing there. Then there's Isla Talamanca. They've got a Club Med there. Southwest there's Sorna. Another company owns that. And up north there's Morazan. It's owned by a rich Costa Rican family. There's nothing on these islands. Even Biosyn saw nothing."

Levine looked up sharply. "Biosyn? Who are they?"

"An American company, in genetics, like InGen. For some reason they're looking for large animals in the forest."

"I wonder why?" Levine said.

"I don't know, Richard," said Marty. "But things are changing. Scientists used to come to study the rain forest because they cared about the natural world. Now they come to get rich. Something new can mean a lot of money. Maybe a new medicine can be made from a new plant, or a spider, or a bird egg. That's probably what Biosyn's after."

Levine's flight was called. The two men stood up.

"You'll keep what you saw today to yourself, Richard?"

"I don't know what I saw today," Levine said.

Marty smiled. "Safe flight, Richard."

♦

Levine walked away, taking his ticket out of his bag. He passed a row of phones. Three people were nodding their heads and talking in Spanish. A fourth person was speaking in English. It was the helicopter pilot.

Levine moved closer. He heard the pilot say, "No, no – no pictures. And I think he knows nothing. He leaves tonight. Yes, it is an island, but which one? We must wait. *Adiós.*"

Levine turned his back as the pilot walked away.

Yes, it is an island, but which one?

Levine had been working day and night on this problem too. He opened his cell-phone and called a number.

"Leave your message," said a voice.

Levine spoke quickly. He reported what he had seen on the beach, and where it was. Then he added, "I'm sending you a small piece of the skin to be studied. I also think some other people are interested. We need to move faster, Ian."

Levine turned the phone off and thought about what Marty had told him. He looked at his ticket. Maybe it was time to change his plan.

Chapter 3   A Lost World

Lewis Dodgson liked to have meetings in the middle of the night. This one was in an empty restaurant. The coffee was bad, but Dodgson didn't care. With him was a heavy man called George Baselton. They were waiting for Ed James.

Dodgson worked for Biosyn. They liked him because he always had good ideas about making money for the company, but his ways were not honest. That's why he needed George's good name. Baselton was a well-known university scientist, paid by Biosyn to make their science reports look clean.

When Ed James arrived, he looked tired. Dodgson paid him five hundred dollars a week to follow a bunch of scientists around. One of the scientists was Richard Levine.

"I don't have all night," said Dodgson. "Let's get started. Any news on the guys who used to work for InGen?"

"Not much," James said, and made his report. Then he added, "InGen is finally selling off its old stuff – cars, computers, nothing interesting."

"Any stuff from Site B?" asked Baselton.

"No idea. I've never heard of Site B before," James said.

"What about Levine?" Dodgson said.

"Levine's ordered special equipment from a company called Thorne Field Systems. It's a small company that makes things for scientists going to rough places. Levine often drives down there in his Ferrari. That's how he got to be a school teacher."

Baselton smiled. "A school teacher?"

"Yes. He was caught speeding right in front of the school near Thorne's factory. The law took his car and his driving papers and told him to teach a class at the school. He seems to like it – he's pretty regular, or was."

"Was?"

"He left the country two days ago. Short trip to Costa Rica, coming back this morning, but he didn't arrive."

"Where is he then?"

"My contact in Costa Rica says he left his hotel. Went to the airport, but didn't take any flight. He's disappeared."

Dodgson looked at him hard. "Find him," he said.

◆

Dr. Levine was talking about meteorites. "What we need to know," he said, "is whether any known worldwide extinctions happened at a time when a giant meteorite hit the earth."

Kelly Curtis watched the TV in front of the class. It showed a field in Manson, Iowa. From the TV, Dr. Levine's voice said, "A meteor fell here, but was it the one that killed the dinosaurs? I'll answer that question next time."

The lights came up and the class was over. Their teacher turned off the computer and the TV.

"Dr. Levine will be with us again after the spring break," she told the class. "Is that right, Kelly and Arby?"

Kelly looked at Arby. "Yes, Mrs. Menzies," she said.

Kelly and Arby had a special job, working for Dr. Levine. They liked going outside school to do things for him.

After class, Arby asked Kelly, "Why isn't he here today?"

"I don't know," said Kelly. "Maybe something happened."

"But he promised to be here," said Arby. "To take us on the tests. It was all planned. And our parents said yes."

Arby's mother and father were busy doctors. Arby was black and very smart, specially with computers. He was only eleven, the youngest in the class – and the shortest.

Kelly was thirteen, and with Arby she always felt tall and messy. Arby's parents made sure he dressed very neatly, but Kelly had to wear her elder sister's old clothes. Her mother was never at home, so Kelly washed her own clothes, but they never looked new, like Arby's. She was sometimes jealous of R. B. Benton, but he was her only real friend.

"Never mind, Arb," she said, "Let's go see Dr. Thorne."

Outside the school they saw the same gray car they had seen, now and again, for the past two months. The man in the car had been following Dr. Levine ever since he started to teach at the school. Was he the reason why Dr. Levine asked them to help him? The man never seemed to notice the kids.

◆

12

Outside the school they saw the same gray car they had seen, now and again, for the past two months.

Levine's message said YOU WERE WRONG. Malcolm found it inside the packet from Costa Rica, with a small piece of green skin. Malcolm sent the skin to a good friend at the zoo, and now he was waiting for her report.

He stood, and walked around the room. He didn't use his stick. He had changed his mind about the possibility of a Lost World, and he wanted to be ready for the expedition, so every day he practiced walking without the stick.

"Malcolm?" said his friend. "Sorry to keep you waiting." She took Malcolm to her office and showed him some large photos of the skin. She said, "It looks like lizard skin, but it seems to be from a warm-blooded animal, perhaps a bird. We don't understand what it is. Can you get more?"

"I might be able to," said Malcolm.

"Where, from Site B?"

"Malcolm looked surprised. "Site B?"

"Well, that's what we can read on this bit of metal on the skin," she said, showing him another large photograph. "You see? Was this animal from a zoo?"

"I don't think so," said Malcolm. "Why do you say that?"

"Because all zoos put metal nameplates like this on young animals."

Malcolm left as soon as he could. He wanted to get to a phone quickly. Outside the zoo he called Levine's number, but Levine wasn't there.

♦

Richard Levine stopped climbing for a moment. The bag on his back was heavy. Far below him was the sea, loud and rough against the rocks. A boat was disappearing in the distance. The sailors who brought him here could not wait in the rough sea. Levine took a deep breath and continued climbing up the steep side of the island.

As he reached the top, the wind pulled at his clothes. One

last deep breath and he was over the edge, lying in soft, wet grass. He looked around – just as he imagined. This was a lost world in the middle of the Pacific Ocean.

He listened to the sound of the wind in the forest. He heard another sound, distant, like the cry of a bird, but deeper. He took his gun out of his bag and put it together. When it was ready he got to his feet and started walking.

Soon he had no view. The forest was dark. Some of the plants were as long and wide as a man's body, and high above them were giant trees.

He walked downhill to a stream, and when he climbed up the other side there was a break in the trees. From here he could see the rocky edge of the west side of the island.

From somewhere in the forest below he heard another deep cry. After a moment the cry was answered. The tops of the forest trees moved, and then it was silent again.

Levine walked down another hill and found another stream. He saw the marks of a small animal in the mud. Something was moving in the grass. Levine stayed very still, waiting. An animal the size of a mouse came out. Levine looked at it, trying not to breathe. Greenish skin without hair, large eyes, like a lizard but . . . was it a *mussaurus*? Levine knew about this small animal from its bones, but now he was looking at a real, living dinosaur!

The little animal came closer. It had a long, thick tail and stood on its strong back legs, waving its little arms in the air. Then suddenly it made an angry little noise and jumped away, disappearing into the forest.

Levine was surprised, then suddenly afraid. Behind him there was a heavy sound, and he noticed a bad smell. He realized, almost too late, that where small animals come to drink, large animals come to kill. He jumped up and ran, but behind him the forest began to shake with terrible cries. In that moment he realized that all his clever planning had gone badly wrong, and he was about to die.

♦

When Kelly and Arby arrived at Thorne's factory, Doc Thorne was standing in the middle of the room, waving his arms and shouting. He never stopped moving. He was a strong, big-chested man of fifty-five, and he was a brilliant engineer.

Around him, mechanics were finishing Levine's expedition orders. There was a big green car – a Ford Explorer – with an electric motor. Its roof was fitted with special glass for making electricity from the sun's heat. There were also two trailers. The bigger one – called "Challenger" – was for working and living in, and for pulling the smaller one, which carried all kinds of equipment, even TVs and a motorcycle. High above them, the head mechanic was working on a kind of cage.

"So where's Levine?" Thorne asked the kids.

"We don't know," Arby said.

"What do you mean? Didn't he teach your class today?"

"No, he didn't come."

"Well, I need him today," Thorne said loudly, "to plan the final tests. He was supposed to be back today."

"Back from where?" Kelly said.

"Oh, somewhere," Thorne said. "He didn't want to say. I gave him my latest phone equipment. He liked it."

Suddenly, the large metal cage came crashing down.

"Eddie," shouted Thorne. "What are you doing up there?"

"Sorry, Doc," called Eddie. "Just testing."

"Okay, Eddie, but don't test when we're under it." Thorne bent to look at the cage, which was round and made of light metal. It was not damaged. He lifted it with one hand and said, "You see? Very light. Like that tall platform there."

"What's it for?"

"I don't know," Thorne said. "But like everything else he wants it strong and light. I can build it strong. I can build it light. But strong and light? It's impossible, what he's asking for, but we're doing it anyway."

"About that phone," Arby said. "Where can he use it?"

"Anywhere in the world," said Thorne.

"But isn't it heavy?" asked Arby.

"Come and see," Thorne said, and took them to his office. He began to explain about his special phone when it rang. Thorne answered. Nothing. Then some noise. "Richard?" said Thorne. "Richard? It's Thorne. Push the T switch to talk!"

Then there was a lot of noise and a voice, very distant, said, "Hello? This is Levine. Can you hear me? Listen. I need help. I'm on the island. I got here all right but . . ."

There was a lot of noise, then they heard, ". . . very serious . . . want to kill me . . . can smell them . . . night . . . please!" And suddenly the phone went dead.

Thorne turned to the kids. Their faces were white. "We have to find him," he said. "But where is he?"

Chapter 4   Which Island?

Thorne unlocked the door to Levine's apartment and put on the lights. They stared. It was full of valuable things, all in plastic cases. Everything was very neat and clean.

They all began to search around. Kelly looked through some papers by the telephone and found a note in Levine's hand-writing. It said: "Site B = Nublar? 1 of 5 Deaths?"

"You better come in here," said Arby from the next room.

Levine's office was also very neat. There was a desk, a computer under a plastic cover, and neat piles of books and papers. On the wall behind the desk was a big board, with maps, photographs and a note that said, "Site B? WHERE???" Arby said, "What's Site B? He really wants to find it."

Near the note there was a photo of a man in a forest. He was standing by a wooden sign that said "SITE B," and he was wearing a white coat with "InGen" on the pocket.

Under the photo was a page cut from a company report. Levine had put a circle around these words:

> As well as its head office in Palo Alto, California, InGen has three science stations around the world, one in South Africa, one in the mountains of Costa Rica, and one on the island of Nublar, 120 miles west of Costa Rica.

On the report Levine had written, "Nublar NOT Site B."

"He thinks Site B's on an island somewhere," Arby said.

"He said he's on an island now," Kelly said.

"But which one?" Thorne said, looking at all the maps.

Another piece of paper had a strange message on it:

> SITE B @#$#TO ALL DEPARTMENTS OF[] ~~Mr. Hammond has~~ ✳✳✳✳ after "✳"market ✳%✳✳ planning ✳✳% Mr. Hammond will ~~not~~ give no information to the public about Isla S work program at any time $%

Arby looked at it thoughtfully.

"Does it make any sense to you?" Thorne asked.

"Yes," Arby said. He pulled the cover off Levine's computer and said, "I thought so."

The computer was large and heavy – not at all modern. On it was a small metal sign that said "InGen, Palo Alto, CA."

"What's this," Thorne said, "an InGen computer?"

"Yes," Arby said. "They were selling off this stuff last week. Dr. Levine sent us to buy it."

"But why would he want this old thing," Thorne asked.

"He didn't tell us," Arby said, turning on the computer. "But I know now. That message – you know why it looks that way? It's an old computer report. Dr. Levine got it from the memory in this machine. Let's have a look."

Arby began to type at the computer. A message came up:

TOTAL REPORTS IN MEMORY: 2,387

The computer was large and heavy—not at all modern. On it was a small metal sign that said "InGen, Palo Alto, CA."

"Thorne said, "More than two thousand! How can you –?"

"Give me a minute here, Doc," Arby said, typing faster.

◆

Returning from the zoo, Malcolm thought about dinosaurs. Back in the 1840s when Richard Owen first described giant bones in England he named them *Dinosauria*: terrible lizards. It's still the best way to describe them, Malcolm thought. They *were* like lizards, and they *were* terrible.

In the 19th century people thought of dinosaurs as fat, slow, weak and stupid, which was why they became extinct. That view didn't change until the 1960s, when a few scientists suggested they were quick and hot-blooded. And now the idea was growing that they were good, caring, family animals which were killed by a meteor.

This view made Malcolm angry. Life always has two faces. Some dinosaurs were peaceful animals, living in groups, caring for their babies. But others were terrible killers.

Malcolm was worried about the piece of metal on the dead animal Levine had seen. He was sure it meant trouble.

Back in his office he called Levine's number again. The phone rang. The answering machine was still on.

Malcolm said, "Richard, if you're there, pick up, please!"

He waited. Nothing happened.

"Richard, it's Ian. Listen, we have a problem. I've had a report on that skin. Richard, it may help us find Site B."

He heard someone lift the phone. "Richard?" he said.

"No," said a voice. "This is Thorne. You'd better get over here right away."

◆

Coming into the apartment, Malcolm said, "I knew it. Richard can't wait. He always has to be first."

"Do you know which island he's on?" Thorne asked.

"Not exactly," Malcolm said. "But our information suggested it was one of five islands in the southwest."

Thorne pointed to a map. "These islands here?"

"Yes," said Malcolm. "They're about ten miles from Puerto Cortéz. Nobody lives there. Local people call them the Five Deaths. Their names are Matanceros, Muerte, Tacaño, Sorna and Pena – all names of death and destruction."

"And which one is Site B?" Arby asked from the computer.

Malcolm turned quickly. "What do you know about Site B?"

"Nothing," Arby said. "But Dr. Levine was looking for Site B, and that name comes up in these reports."

Malcolm went to look over Arby's shoulder.

"These are InGen reports," said Arby. "Look."

Malcolm studied the computer reports. Some of them said Site B, but nothing was very clear. Then, in a list of names and numbers, Malcolm saw GAS LINES and GAS STATION.

"If this means Site B had gas," he said, "I think we can choose the right island right now."

◆

Ed James heard these words, and sat up in his car. He was parked across the street from Levine's apartment building. His listening equipment was working fine.

One of the kids said, "How?"

James felt foolish. So the kids were working for Levine! He had seen them often – a short black boy and a tall white girl, maybe eleven or twelve. But it didn't matter now.

"The gas is from a dead volcano," he heard Malcolm say. "So it's this island here. This is where Levine is."

The girl said, "You think so? Isla Sorna?"

James wrote ISLA SORNA in his notebook.

"That's our island," said Thorne. "Let's go, kids."

They all left the building. Ed picked up his phone.

◆

Back at the factory, the workers were gone and everything was finished. Eddie Carr, the head mechanic, was waiting.

"Some of the paint is still a bit wet, Doc," he said, "but we're ready for the test trip tomorrow."

"We're not going on a test trip," Thorne said. "We're going on a real trip. And we're not going tomorrow – we're going tonight."

"Great," said Arby. "Where are we going?"

"Isla Sorna," Thorne said. "And you're not coming."

"But our parents said yes," Arby said.

"They said yes to a test trip near here," Thorne said. "Not to a real trip in Costa Rica. Now Eddie, we need to get all this stuff into the containers. Call the airport. I want to be off the ground in four hours. And pack a bag, Eddie, you're coming with me!"

"So are we," Kelly said.

"No way, kids," Thorne said. "It's too dangerous. Now where's Malcolm? We need to call Sarah Harding in Africa."

Kelly's eyes widened. "Sarah Harding? Is she coming too?"

"I don't know," Thorne said, and hurried away.

"Who is she?" Arby asked.

"Only the best young animal scientist in the world, Arb." Sarah Harding was one of Kelly's personal heroes. Kelly had read everything she could about her. Like Kelly, Harding came from a poor family. Now, at thirty-three, she was a top scientist. She was beautiful, independent and famous.

"Never heard of her," said Arby. "But if *she's* going . . ."

◆

"We need to talk about the future," Dodgson told his boss.

Lewis Dodgson was forty-five years old. His face was pink and his hair was thinning. He had a pleasant smile but he was not a pleasant person. He was a scientist in a hurry, and he was ready to do anything to get results.

Jeff Rossiter, the head of the Biosyn company, looked at his watch. "It's late, Lew," he said. "Get it out."

"I'll come right to the point," Dodgson said. "If we move quickly we have a chance to carry on where InGen stopped."

"Dinosaurs?" Rossiter said. "What do we want dinosaurs for?"

"For animal testing," Dodgson said. "It's getting harder and harder to test new medicines on animals. These days, everybody loves animals. You can't test them, you can't shoot them, some people don't even want you to eat them. But nobody loves dinosaurs – they don't exist, do they? So if we make them exist, people can't complain."

Rossiter was shaking his head.

"Come on, Jeff. Think about it. In the future we can test medicines on small dinosaurs instead of dogs and rats."

Rossiter looked up at Dodgson. "You can get dinosaurs?"

Dodgson nodded.

"Okay," Rossiter said. "Do it."

Chapter 5   Site B

From the first helicopter, Thorne could see five islands.

"We call them the Five Deaths," said the pilot.

Sorna was the biggest island. From above, it was clearly an old volcano, with high rock walls and a deep center. Thorne looked down to the crashing sea below.

"Where do boats land?" he asked.

The pilot pointed to the east side. "In good weather a boat can pass through caves, made by the sea."

Thinking of Sarah Harding, Thorne said, "Another scientist may arrive later today. Can you bring her out?"

"I'm sorry," the pilot said. "We have another job. But if the sea is calm she can get a boat. She may have luck."

"And you will come back for us early tomorrow morning?"

"Yes, Señor Thorne. It's the best time, for the winds."

♦

The two helicopters lifted off the ground and disappeared into the sky. Malcolm sat quietly in the morning heat, as Eddie Carr and Thorne opened the containers. Eddie drove the Explorer to where the sun could fall on the glass roof. He checked the electric motor – it was fine. Thorne checked the Challenger, then joined it up to the second trailer, locking them together with a strong metal bridge. They put the motorbike on the back of the Explorer.

Finally, Thorne got out two guns – very big air guns used to shoot poison into wild animals. "Just remember," he told Malcolm and Eddie, "don't shoot yourself in the foot with one of these, or you'll be dead before you know it!"

Malcolm took one of the guns. Thorne handed the other gun to Eddie and said, "Let's get going."

Eddie climbed into the Explorer. Thorne and Malcolm climbed into the Challenger. A moment later, the radio came on. Eddie said, "You getting the TV system ready, Doc?"

"Yeah. Right now," Thorne said, and Malcolm saw the island appear on the small TV in front of him.

The same thing came on the TV in the Explorer.

Thorne pressed a button and the computer made the picture clearer. Malcolm could see a map of lines and a red X.

"That's us," Thorne said, pointing at the X.

"Okay," Eddie said, on the radio. "I've got it. Looks like a road going north. That where we're going?"

"I'd say so," Thorne said. "You go first, Eddie."

"Okay, Doc. Here we go."

They drove away from the landing place into thick forest. After ten minutes they came to a small stream, with muddy

24

banks. The Explorer started across it, then stopped. Eddie got out and walked back, stepping over rocks in the water.

"I saw something, Doc," he said.

The others got out of the Challenger and stood on the banks of the stream. They heard distant cries in the trees.

"Birds?" Thorne said, but Malcolm shook his head.

Eddie picked up something green, and said, "This is a piece from the bag we made for Levine, Doc." He turned to show it to Doc. "Uh-oh," he said. "We have company."

Near the Challenger there was a group of about six bright-green lizards. They stood up on their back legs with their tails straight out. They were about the size of chickens, and when they walked their heads went up and down quickly, exactly like chickens. They looked at the men with their heads on one side and made bird-like noises.

"*Compys*," said Malcolm. "*Procompsognathus triassicus*."

"You mean these are –?"

"Yes. They're dinosaurs."

Eddie stared. "I didn't know they came so small."

"Dinosaurs were mostly small," Malcolm said. "People always think they were enormous, but mostly they were the size of a sheep, or a very small horse."

"They look like chickens," Eddie said.

"Is there any danger?" Thorne asked.

"Not really. They don't kill. They feed on dead animals. But don't get close. Their bite can be poisonous."

"Why aren't they afraid?" Eddie asked, picking up a rock.

"Hey!" Malcolm said. "Don't do that."

But Eddie threw the rock. A few of the *compys* moved away quickly, but the others stayed where they were.

"They have a bad smell," Eddie said. "Like something dead. And it's not natural, not being frightened of us."

They returned to the cars and drove on. Eddie was worried about the cars. Over the radio he said, "Why didn't we test first,

25

But nobody saw the view. What they saw were some large animals walking slowly across the road.

Doc? You don't come to a place with poisonous chickens if you don't test your cars first."

"The cars are fine," Thorne said.

They followed the rough road up a hill, and came to a place where the road had two branches. An old wooden sign pointed one way to RIVER and the other way to SITE B.

Eddie said, "Guys? Which way?"

"Go to Site B," Malcolm said.

They took the road on the right and drove on, then suddenly the Explorer stopped. Thorne nearly hit it.

"Hey!" he said. "What now, Eddie?"

Eddie was staring along the road to a place where the trees were clear, and there was a view right across the island to the west. But nobody saw the view. What they saw were some large animals walking slowly across the road.

"*Triceratops*," Malcolm said.

The group calmly crossed the road and passed down the hill. Then the men looked at the view – a green valley with a river. On both sides of the river, animals were eating. About twenty dark-green dinosaurs moved slowly through the deep grass as they ate. Eight others with strange heads drank from the river. The group of *triceratops* moved slowly past a *stegosaurus*. A dozen long-necked *apatosaurs* were lazily eating the tops of trees. It was a peaceful scene.

Eddie said, "What *is* this place?"

"I think Site B might give us an answer," said Malcolm.

The Explorer and the two trailers continued along the road. First they came to a small building that looked like a guardhouse. Soon they came to a second guardhouse, and then, around a bend, they saw Site B spread out below them.

In the center there was an enormous building with a flat roof – it was the size of two football fields. Behind it was a tall building with a metal roof. Thorne thought it could be an electricity station – big enough for a small town! There were places for turning and parking trucks.

"Do you know what this is?" Thorne asked Malcolm.

"Yes," Malcolm said, nodding slowly. "It's a factory."

Over the radio, Eddie said, "What do you want to do?"

"We'll park the trailers over there," Thorne said, "then we'll have a look around. I think he'll be here somewhere."

They parked the trailers and climbed into the Explorer.

"Let's go find Levine," Thorne said, and they drove off.

Chapter 6   A Good Parent

It was silent inside the Challenger. The switches and buttons in front of the driving seat shone bright green, and the red X on the TV showed clearly. Then a noise came from the back, where the kitchen and beds were. The door of a high cupboard opened, and a pile of blankets fell out onto the floor. Out of the blankets climbed Arby Benton. "If I don't go to the toilet I'm going to *scream*," he said.

It was Arby who planned how they could hide in the trailer. He knew it would be cold in the plane, so he got out all the blankets. He knew it would take twelve hours, so he made sure they had plenty of cookies and water. But he forgot about the toilet! He hurried there now.

From under the bed there was a shout. "I have to *go*," Kelly said, climbing out of her blankets and following him.

Arby came out of the bathroom with a big smile and said, "We did it! We're here."

"Just a minute, Arb. Okay?"

Through a window, Arby saw Thorne, Malcolm and Eddie disappearing into a big building. Kelly came back.

"They'll be mad when they find us," Arby said.

"Maybe," Kelly said. "But we're here to help them find

28

Dr. Levine. Arb, were they talking about dinosaurs back there?"

"Couldn't hear," Arby said. "Now let's find some food."

♦

Malcolm, Thorne and Eddie stood in the entrance of the main building. On the wall a sign said WE MAKE THE FUTURE. "It's an InGen building," Thorne said, looking at the sign.

In the dust on the floor were the marks of boots. Thorne pointed to a coffee table near some seats. On it were two empty water bottles, a cell-phone and a torn green bag. Eddie walked over to look at the bag. A large rat jumped out. "Candies," he said. "But nobody will want them now."

They moved on, through some offices with desks, and maps on the wall. There were animal droppings on the floor. Then they passed through some big glass doors.

"What was this building used for?" Thorne asked Malcolm.

"It was a factory for dinosaurs," Malcolm said.

"Why would anybody want that?" Eddie said.

"Nobody would," Malcolm said. "That's why it was secret. It all began like this. A man called John Hammond discovered how to make extinct animals from cells. He decided to make a kind of zoo for tourists, and he called it Jurassic Park. He built his park on an island called Isla Nublar, north of here, and he planned to open it in late 1989. I went to see it just before the opening. But it never happened. Hammond had problems with the park systems. The dinosaurs escaped, and some visitors were killed, so the park and all its dinosaurs were destroyed."

They came to a window where they could look out over the river. Thorne watched the dinosaurs, eating peacefully, and said, "If they were all destroyed, what's this island?"

"This island," Malcolm said, "is Hammond's dirty secret. He pretended to make his dinosaurs at the park. Tourists could

29

watch the babies come out of perfect eggs. But for every good egg there were many bad ones. Hammond didn't want to show that, so the eggs were actually made here."

"If the animals at the zoo were destroyed," Eddie said, "why weren't they destroyed on this island too?"

"A good question," Malcolm said.

♦

Arby was bored. He went to the front of the trailer and looked at the buttons and lights. He picked up the radio and said, "This is Arby. Is anybody there?"

Nobody answered, so he switched on the computer. First he saw **THORNE FIELD SYSTEMS** and a list. From the list he chose **RADIO SYSTEMS**. The computer showed a lot of lines and words, and then nothing. Then one word came up: **PASS-WORD**.

That was odd. Why did Thorne need a special word to get into his own computer systems? Arby tried **THORNE**, then **DOC**, then **THORNE FIELD SYSTEMS**. Nothing. Then he tried **HELP**. Something appeared. "Good," Arby said, smiling happily.

♦

They came to another room, with rows and rows of metal boxes. In one corner there was some old, yellow computer paper. Malcolm looked at it and saw numbers and letters – something about dinosaur blood, he thought. There was also a pile of old messages, all short. He read a few and said, "I think they had problems."

He showed Thorne a longer message. "It seems that the newborn animals were getting sick and dying – something wrong in the factory food. So they decided to let them loose on the island to eat natural food."

"They must have been mad," Eddie said.

"Well, they wanted them back for the park," Malcolm said. "So they put metal nameplates on them and used radio to find them again when they were big enough. Look up there."

A sign on the wall said **BE CLEAN AND CAREFUL STOP DX NOW!**

"I think DX is the name of the sickness," Malcolm said.

They went on, into a enormous room with large machines.

"Hey!" Eddie said.

Malcolm saw it too. It was in the far corner of the room, a small blue box halfway up the wall, with lines running into it. On the box was a small red light.

"A light!" Eddie said. "This place has electricity!"

♦

Arby watched white letters slowly appear on the computer.

DO YOU WANT A PASSWORD?

YES, he typed.

YOUR FULL NAME?

He typed in his name.

After a moment: **YOUR NEW PASSWORD IS VIG/&✳849/.**

Arby wrote it on a piece of paper.

PLEASE ENTER YOUR PASSWORD NOW.

He did. The computer was strangely slow, he thought. Then suddenly the colour changed to dark blue, and he read: **INTERNATIONAL GENETICS: SITE B COMPUTER SYSTEM.**

It didn't make any sense. InGen closed Site B years ago. How could the computer system be here still? And how could he get into it? By radio? But where was the electricity?

Arby waited, and then he saw a list with dates. All 1989. So it really was an old system. No changes since 1989. Did it still work? He decided to try something, so he chose **TV SYSTEM.** And to his surprise, little pictures began to come, fifteen of

*To his surprise, little pictures began to come, fifteen of them, showing
different parts of the island.*

them, showing different parts of the island. Most of the cameras seemed to be high up, and they showed . . .

He stared. *They showed dinosaurs.*

It wasn't possible. They must be old movies – dinosaur movies. But then, in one of the pictures, Arby saw the two trailers parked together. And in another picture he saw Thorne and Malcolm and Eddie get quickly into the Explorer and drive around the back of the big building. And he realized with a shock: *The pictures were all real.*

◆

The men drove the Explorer to the tall building which looked like an electricity station. It had no windows and a heavy metal door with a sign that said DANGER.

They jumped out of the car, and Eddie pushed opened the door. Inside they saw a lot of pipes, and steam was coming out of the floor. It was very hot and quite noisy.

"Wonderful," Eddie said. "The island's a volcano, right? They found a place where steam comes up. They use the steam to turn the machines to make electricity. It's . . ."

Eddie stopped suddenly and hurried back to the Explorer.

". . . into the car!" said a voice from the radio.

"Who is this?" Eddie said.

"It's Arby. Get into the car."

"Who?" Thorne said. "Arby? He's not here, is he?"

"Yes, I'm here," said Arby. "Please get in the car! It's coming. I can see it on TV."

"What does he mean, TV?" Thorne said angrily.

Eddie said, "I don't know, Doc, but if he can see it, we can see it too." He switched on the TV in the Explorer. It showed the enormous body of a *tyrannosaurus rex* moving quickly towards the electricity station. Its skin was reddish brown, the color of dried blood. It passed out of the TV picture but now they could feel the ground shaking.

Staring, Thorne said, "Everybody in the car."

A few minutes later, the animal came out of the trees on the right of the Explorer. It moved quickly past the front of the car and disappeared into the trees on the left. So fast! They only had time to see it was the size of a big building, its head high above them, something in its mouth, its thick tail moving from side to side as it hurried away.

"Are you okay, Dr. Thorne?" said Arby on the radio.

"Yes, Arby. Thanks to you," he said.

"I can see Dr. Levine now," said Arby. "He's riding a bicycle. He's following the dinosaur in the forest."

"I'm going after him," Thorne said. "Get down the motorbike, Eddie."

◆

Levine was in a very good place to watch the *tyrannosaurs*. There was no question: this was their nest. They were enormous. They moved slowly, almost gently, passing bits of red meat to their young.

Arby could see the nest too, on the television. Kelly watched with him. In the nest were four white eggs, about the size of footballs. There were also some bits of broken egg and two babies, opening their mouths for food.

Kelly loved the dinosaurs. She wanted to get out of the trailer as soon as possible. Arby felt safer inside.

"Look, Kel," he said. "Dr. Thorne is there now. He's pushing the motorbike. Probably wants to keep quiet."

Thorne saw the bicycle under a tree. It had "InGen" painted on it. On the radio, Arby said, "He's in the tree."

Thorne looked up. He couldn't see Levine, but he could hear a lot of noise. Then suddenly, with a loud crash, Levine fell out of the tree. He looked up and smiled. "What a surprise, Doc," he said.

"Oh, no!" Kelly said, watching the television. The two

tyrannosaurs were moving quickly in circles, lifting their heads and waving their tails over the babies in the nest.

"Get out of there right now," said Arby, on the radio.

Thorne jumped on the motorcycle and started the engine. Levine jumped on behind him. They heard a terrible cry, and looked back to see one of the *tyrannosaurs* crash through the trees at full speed. Thorne could feel the ground shake. The noise hurt his ears. He drove away fast.

"Take it easy, Doc," Levine shouted.

Thorne took no notice. He drove faster and faster.

"Are you trying to kill us, Doc? We're alone."

Thorne looked back. Levine was right. He slowed the bike. "He just wanted to frighten us off," Levine said. "He's gone back to his nest."

"Then I guess we're lucky he's a good parent," said Doc.

◆

"Of course the *tyrannosaur* is a good parent," Levine said, when they got back to the trailers. "Didn't you see how thin he was? He's feeding his young and not feeding himself. Next, he'll teach them to find their own food. He'll start by bringing in live animals for them to kill."

"Thorne saved your life, Richard," Malcolm said.

"No, he didn't," Levine said. "There was no danger. Except when he was driving." He looked at the angry faces all around him. "But why are you all here? And the kids?"

Eddie said, "We all came here to save you."

"I don't know why," Levine said. "I never asked you to."

"On the phone . . ." Arby said.

"We heard you . . ." Kelly said.

"That was a mistake," Levine said. "I was up in a tree, and there were eight hungry *velociraptors* jumping around, trying to get me. They left me alone in the morning. But the expedition

is here now, so everything's fine, isn't it? We've got a lot to do
– and I think we should get started."

Chapter 7   Killing Machine

It was eleven o'clock in the morning and Sarah Harding was
still trying to get to Isla Sorna. After fifteen hours traveling she
was tired and dirty, and now there was no helicopter to take her
from Puerto Cortés to the island.

She was watching the boats in the little fishing port. Most
were tied up and silent, but there were signs of life around the
largest one. Two Americans were shouting and pointing as a
red Jeep Wrangler was lifted on to the boat.

"Careful! Careful!" shouted one of the men.

Harding went over to him and said, "Excuse me. My name's
Sarah Harding and I'm trying to get to . . ."

"I don't care who you are," said the man, rudely.

"I'm trying to get to Isla Sorna," she said, finishing.

At this the man's face changed. "Isla Sorna?" he said. "You
aren't working with Dr. Levine, by any chance?"

"Yes, I am."

"What do you know!" he said with a big smile. "I'm Lew
Dodgson, from Biosyn, and this is George Baselton."

Harding recognized Baselton, of course, but was surprised to
find him here. "Are you friends of Richard?" she asked.

"We're on our way to see him right now," Dodgson said,
"to help him out. You're welcome to join us. Climb up."

♦

The boat was nearing the island. Dodgson seemed very
friendly now. Baselton had disappeared – seasick perhaps.

"Tell me about Biosyn," she said.

"It's a small company," Dodgson said. "We make animals for

36

modern needs – new kinds of dogs, smaller pets for city people, for example. And you?"

"I work in Africa," she said. "Doc Thorne called me yesterday and I left immediately. Are they there now?"

"Who?"

"Doc and Ian Malcolm."

"Yes – yes, they are. Do they know you're coming?"

"Not really," Harding said. "I just promised to try to get there."

The sea was getting rough as they came near the island. Then a big wave came over the boat. "Don't be frightened," Dodgson said with a smile, and he pushed her into the sea.

♦

The metal cage was lying in the grass. Above it, the tall platform was hidden among some trees.

"This is called a high hide," said Levine. "We're safe up here, or we can lock ourselves in the cage if we need to."

Thorne, Eddie, Malcolm and the kids were all with Levine on the platform. The noon air was hot and sticky. Down below, the valley was quiet. Some *apatosaurs* were drinking from the river. Near them were some *parasaurolophasaurs*.

"That's very interesting," Levine said. "They help each other. The *apatosaurs* have weak eyes. The *parasaurs* are guarding them. Now watch that *raptor*."

On the other side of the river, a lizard-like dinosaur came out of the trees. It was green-brown with red lines.

"That's what chased you up the tree, Levine?" asked Doc.

"That's it," Levine said. "*Velociraptor*. That one will be the leader. They work together like a killing machine."

The *parasaurs* began crying loudly, moving closer to the *apatosaurs*. As more *raptors* came out of the trees, the *apatosaurs* turned their backs and moved their enormously strong tails

The parasaurs *began crying loudly, moving closer to the* apatosaurs.

from side to side. The long tails reached right across the river. The *raptors* turned away.

"They're afraid of those tails," Thorne said.

"We need to know where their nest is, Ian," Levine said. "Want to follow them in the Explorer?"

"Not now," Malcolm said, "If Sarah is coming we should be there to meet her. Let's go back to the trailers."

"Okay," Levine said. "You go. But I'm staying here."

◆

Sarah Harding was lying in mud, too tired to move. She remembered swimming through a dark cave into a wide, sunny river. Further up the river she could see Dodgson's boat tied up, but it was empty. Now she just wanted to sleep.

She lay on her back and closed her eyes. It was hot, and the ground was shaking gently. She dreamed of a horse, a horse with a big, soft eye and a warm, wet tongue. The tongue was on her neck, moving up her cheek. It was quite a nice feeling but – it wasn't a horse!

She sat up suddenly and looked into the face of – a *stegosaurus*! It moved back in surprise, then slowly began to drink from the river. She moved away from its enormous feet, stood up, and started walking.

◆

"I told you, George, it was an accident," Dodgson said. "A big wave came and she was washed off the boat. We looked for her, but there was no hope. Now pass me that box."

Baselton passed the box. They were sitting in the forest in the Jeep Wrangler. They were near a dinosaur nest.

"We have to get eggs from the nest, George," he said.

"But we can't do that," Baselton said. "They'll kill us."

"Not with this box," Dodgson said, and got out of the car. Baselton followed. They moved forward quietly until, through the leaves, they could see a clear area and about twenty light-colored adult dinosaurs.

"*Maiasaurs*," whispered Dodgson. "The name means good-mother lizard. Plant-eaters. No problems here."

"The *maiasaurs* certainly were behaving like good parents, dropping grass on their eggs to keep them warm.

"They're just big, stupid cows," Dodgson said. "Ready?"

He stepped into the nest with the box and switched it on. A terrible, high noise came out. The *maiasaurs* found the noise painful to their ears. They moved away. Baselton followed quickly, took an egg and returned to the car. Dodgson walked back slowly, turning off the box.

"Stupid animals," he said. "Now for the next."

◆

Alone in the high hide, Levine watched the *parasaurs*. Watching was the best part of his work. Malcolm liked to think about theories but Levine liked facts and details.

The *parasaurs* were coming up from the valley in a single line. They passed the high hide. Where were they going? There was only one way to find out. Levine climbed down.

◆

Sarah Harding was very thirsty. The river was below her now, and she seemed to be on an animal path in the forest. In front of her there was the sound of excited animals, maybe dogs, and suddenly a bright green animal crashed through the trees. Something was chasing it.

She jumped into a tree and climbed high. More animals crashed through the trees – dark bodies with red lines. She counted nine as they passed underneath. Then she dropped to the ground and followed them. She wanted to see the kill.

In Africa, animals around a kill behave in a certain way: the killers eat first, with their young, and other birds and animals wait for their turn.

Around this kill there was noise and fighting. The killers were tearing at the meat and biting at each other. Young animals could not get close. One adult was bitten badly. As it moved away, three others jumped on it. Harding closed her eyes and moved away. This was a different world.

♦

Thorne, Malcolm and Eddie ate lunch with Arby and Kelly in the Challenger, then decided to go back to join Levine.

"Kids," Malcolm said, "you stay here and watch the TV."

The Ford Explorer moved quietly through the forest. They were following an animal path above the valley.

"Stop," Malcolm said, suddenly. "Did you hear a car?"

Thorne stopped the engine. They listened in the sticky heat. Then the radio came on. It was Arby, in the trailer.

"Dr. Malcolm? Turn on your television."

Thorne turned it on. The picture showed trees. Through the leaves they saw someone – small body, short dark hair.

"It's Sarah," Malcolm said, smiling.

"Well, we'd better go get her," Thorne said. "I'll tell Richard." He reached for the radio and called Levine.

There was no answer.

"Great," said Malcolm. "Probably gone for a walk."

"That's what I'm afraid of," Thorne said. "Eddie, get down the motorbike and follow Levine. And take a gun."

♦

"*Very* nice," whispered a voice behind Dr. Levine. He turned, and saw Eddie Carr sitting on the motorcycle.

"Sssh," Levine said angrily. "It's very interesting. Don't you see? It's their toilet place."

"It certainly smells like that," Eddie said.

41

The *parasaurs* were leaving now.

"Dr. Levine," Eddie said. "Get on the bike."

Suddenly, dozens of little dinosaurs jumped into the area. Levine bent forward to watch. Interesting. They were eating the fresh droppings of the *parasaurs*.

"Poisonous chickens," Eddie said.

"*Compys*," said Levine, watching carefully. He slowly put out a hand, and one of the *compys* bit it.

"That's enough," Eddie said. "We're leaving *now*."

Chapter 8   Attack

It was mid-afternoon. In the high hide, Eddie cleaned the cut on Levine's hand.

"Stop moving," he said. "It won't take a minute. Then I'm going back. Do you want to come?"

"Certainly not," Levine said. "My work is here."

In the trailers, Sarah Harding was having a shower. Kelly brought her soap, towels, clean clothes – she would do anything to help her hero.

At the front of the Challenger, Thorne, Malcolm and Arby were watching the television. Suddenly, Malcolm said, "There – in a red Jeep. Must be Dodgson. Where are they?"

Arby looked closely. "Near where we found Dr. Levine."

Thorne called Levine on the radio. "We have visitors near the *tyrannosaurs*' nest."

Levine's voice said, "Whatever they're doing, stop them."

"Okay," Thorne said. "Tell Eddie to meet us on the way."

◆

Dodgson stopped the Jeep Wrangler and listened. Something very big, making a noise like a giant cat. Walking. Making everything shake gently. "Come on," he said. "Same again."

He and Baselton got out of the car and walked toward the nest. There were two adults, twenty feet high, strong, dark red, with horribly big teeth. Like the *maiasaurs* they stared at the men for a moment, then gave a terrible cry.

Dodgson lifted the box and pointed it at the animals. The noise started. The animals came forward, but Dodgson stayed cool. He turned the sound higher and they moved back.

Baselton climbed into the nest. He saw four big eggs and two young babies. He picked up an egg but his hands were shaking. The egg flew into the air. As he reached to catch it he stepped on a baby. Screaming in pain and fear, the baby bit Baselton's leg and held on tightly.

Above the noise of the box, the parents heard the scream. "Move," shouted Dodgson, but Baselton could not.

"What are they doing?" Arby cried, in the trailer.

The *tyrannosaurs* moved forward. Holding the box, Dodgson ran to the nest, took the egg and ran back to the car.

The baby screamed louder, and then Dodgson heard a different scream. He looked back and saw something hanging from an enormous mouth. It was Baselton.

Dodgson drove away fast, too fast, and ran the car over the edge of a steep hill. The car stopped. Dodgson fell through trees, hit his head and didn't know anything more.

◆

The Explorer was parked above the nest. Thorne, Malcolm and Harding saw the two animals leave the nest.

"I guess Dodgson took something," Malcolm said.

Eddie arrived. "Are you going down?" he asked.

"No, certainly not. It's too dangerous," Malcolm said.

Sarah Harding said, "What are we carrying?"

Thorne said, "Three guns."

"Okay," she said. "Let's take a quick look."

The nest was quiet.

Nobody thought that Eddie would do what he did. He took the baby tyrannosaur back to the trailers.

"They took one of the eggs," Malcolm said.

"And they hurt a baby," Harding said. "Broken leg."

"Let's go," Thorne said. "Meet us at the trailers, Eddie."

◆

Nobody thought that Eddie would do what he did. He took the baby *tyrannosaur* back to the trailers.

When Levine heard, he called Thorne on the radio. "Bring the kids here," he said. "That baby has very big parents!"

While Harding and Malcolm tried to fix the baby's broken leg, the kids, with Levine, Thorne and Eddie, watched the valley in the evening light. They heard distant thunder.

"I'm glad we're going back in the morning," Arby said.

"Those *triceratops* down at the river," Levine said. "Why have they started moving like that?"

"What's in the trees on the other side?" Arby said.

"I see them," Kelly said. "*Raptors.*"

"I think we're about to see a kill," said Levine happily.

Arby and Kelly stared silently as the *raptors* ran and killed and fought each other among the *triceratops*.

Soon it was night.

"Maybe we should go back now," Eddie said.

"Not yet," Thorne said, and Levine agreed. He had special night glasses for watching in the dark.

◆

In the Challenger, Malcolm and Harding were alone together. The baby's leg was fixed, and they planned to take it back in the morning. They talked about the *raptors*.

"I counted nine," Harding said.

"I counted fourteen," Malcolm said.

"That's too many," Harding said. "In Africa and India, killer animals are very spread out – one for every two hundred other animals. How many animals are there here?"

"Maybe two hundred – at the most five hundred."

"So what other food do the *raptors* eat?"

As she spoke, Levine came on the radio. "I can see you through my night glasses," he said. "Everything all right?"

"Fine," said Malcolm. But it wasn't.

Outside, the two *tyrannosaurs* were looking for their baby. They stood quietly in the trees, smelling and waiting. Then they came closer. The trailers shook, Levine saw them. "Give them the baby," he said on the radio.

Harding took the baby and put it outside the door. The parents came closer and smelt it. They picked it up, took it into the forest, and put it on the ground. Then they turned, gave a terrible cry, and ran toward the trailers.

The crash was terrible. Malcolm hit his head and fell to the floor. Sarah screamed. Then the Challenger started to move. It was pushed, pushed, pushed until it fell over the edge of the hill. Metal screamed and suddenly they were hanging in the air, five hundred feet above the valley.

"Something's happening," Levine said to Thorne. "I can't see the trailers. You'd better go and help."

♦

As Thorne left in the Explorer, the rain started. It fell heavily and noisily on the car, and made the road muddy. Thorne drove fast, but he was worried about the electric motor. Eddie spoke over the radio. "Doc? Are you almost there?"

"Almost, Eddie," Thorne said. And then the car stopped dead. Water had got into the motor. But what was that up the hill on the side of the road? Dodgson's red Jeep! He took the radio and the gun and ran.

There was no time to radio Eddie. The keys were in the Jeep, and he backed it carefully on to the road. Around a few more bends in the road and there it was – Site B – and the dinosaurs were pushing the trailers! In the lights of the Jeep, the dinosaurs stopped and turned. Then they ran to the trees, took their baby and left.

Thorne fixed one end of a rope around a tree and ran to the trailers with the other. The Challenger was hanging over the valley. The second trailer was on the edge, holding the Challenger by the metal bridge between them.

"Can you climb?" Thorne shouted, throwing the rope down.

"I can," called Sarah, but Ian can't. He hit his head."

She tied the rope around Malcolm, and pushed while Thorne pulled. Slowly they lifted him up. Then Sarah climbed up. Behind her, the metal bridge broke and the Challenger fell with a crash into the valley below.

◆

Watching through the night glasses, Levine said, "They're safe!" Kelly laughed, but Arby pointed down to the valley. The *raptors* had crossed the river and were coming up toward the high hide. Twelve of them. Coming nearer.

At first the animals did not seem to notice the hide. Then one stopped and smelt something – a candy, dropped in the grass. It looked up and stared at them. Then it jumped.

Eddie was surprised at how high it jumped – eight feet straight up, again and again. Other *raptors* came back and began to jump too. And they began to learn how to climb.

"Get back," Levine said. "Don't look out."

Eddie picked up a piece of metal from the floor and bent over the side, trying to fight the *raptors* as they climbed. One bit his shirt, and held on. Eddie pushed the metal into its eye and it fell away.

"Up to the roof," Levine shouted to the kids. "Quick!" Eddie fought the animals with the metal. Levine pushed Kelly up, and then helped Arby. "Go on, go on!"

Suddenly there was a terrible cry as Eddie fell to the ground. Immediately the animals dropped to the ground too. They heard Eddie screaming in the night. Then Arby fell.

"Get here! Get here!" shouted Levine into the radio.

♦

Sarah was on the motorcycle in a moment, her gun over her shoulder. Thorne pulled the rope off the Jeep and followed.

♦

Kelly heard Arby shouting, "The key! The key!" From the wet roof she looked down and saw him inside the cage. Three *raptors* were biting and kicking the cage, trying to get at Arby. A young one was trying to bite something around its neck.

As the *raptors* kicked and pushed the cage, it began to move away, faster and faster. The other *raptors* were fighting over Eddie's body. As the lights of the Jeep came closer, they ran off with the body, following the cage.

"They're taking Arby," screamed Kelly, climbing down. Levine was down first and jumped into the Jeep. Kelly jumped on the motorbike behind Sarah. "Take this gun," Sarah said to Kelly. "We're going to need it."

Chapter 9   Three Excited Babies

It was a terrible ride through the forest. The *raptors* ran, carrying Eddie's body and pushing the cage with Arby in it. The Jeep crashed after them over the rough ground.

"You're going to kill us," Levine shouted.

The *raptors* disappeared over a small hill. "I think we've lost them," Levine said. "We have to give up."

"The boy didn't give up on you," Thorne said, angrily. He drove to the top of the hill and stopped to look down.

Levine stared. "I think we've found the *raptors'* nest."

In the nest they could see the cage, but the *raptors* were busy with Eddie's bones. There were other bones too.

"*Apatosaur* bones," Levine said. "Too many!"

"Hold tight," Thorne said. "We're going in to get Arby." He drove fast into the nest, jumped out, threw the cage into the back of the Jeep, and drove out again. For a moment the *raptors* were surprised, then with horrible screams they began to chase the Jeep.

"Get Arby out," shouted Thorne, driving hard.

Levine climbed into the back of the jeep. "I can't," he said. "The cage is locked and the key's gone."

◆

Kelly knew where the key was. Its string was caught around the neck of the young *raptor*. "Follow that one," she shouted to Sarah. "We have to get the key back."

Trying to lose the motorcycle, the animal ran this way and that, but Sarah followed.

"Shoot!" she shouted, when they came close, but Kelly missed. "Shoot again! You can do it." Kelly tried again and missed again.

Kelly knew she must hit the *raptor*. It seemed impossible, but she wanted Sarah to be proud of her.

The *raptor* was running fast, toward the river. The motorbike hit a rock and flew into the air, coming down with a crash. The *raptor* turned, and Sarah brought the bike up very close. Kelly pushed the gun into the animal's neck.

Kelly knew she must hit the raptor. It seemed impossible, but she wanted Sarah to be proud of her.

"Do it," shouted Sarah, and Kelly fired.

The *raptor* ran on, then suddenly fell. Sarah stopped the bike, took the gun and fired again at the silent animal.

"Wait here," she said, and walked over to where it lay in the grass. When she came back, she had the key in her hand.

◆

"Hey, son," said Thorne. "How are you doing in there?"

Arby's face was covered with blood, but he seemed to be able to move. "Been better," he said in a small voice.

"Look," Levine said, pointing behind them. Thorne looked back and saw that the *raptors* were still chasing them. He drove faster, and then, in front, he saw the lights of the bike. He drove past Sarah and she threw him the key.

"Follow me fast," he shouted. "Back to the trailer."

◆

Malcolm was hurt, but he had medicine to take away the pain. "Where have you been?" he asked, when everyone returned to the trailer. "And what's that outside?"

"It's *raptors*," Thorne said. "We can't stay here. This trailer isn't safe. We have to get over to the factory."

"Hey, everybody," Sarah said. "Look who's here."

Kelly helped Arby to come forward. He looked terrible, but he was walking. And he was wearing clean clothes.

Thorne said, "How do you feel, son?"

Arby said, "Everything hurts, but I'm okay. Just hungry."

"Do we have any more guns?" Sarah asked Thorne.

"No," Thorne said, "but we can use this." He showed her a can. "It's gas. If we take out this pin and throw it, the gas will keep the *raptors* quiet for three minutes."

Thorne and Levine got ready to carry Malcolm and Arby.

51

Sarah took out the pin and threw the can. Nothing happened. It just lay in the grass. One of the animals saw it and went over to smell it. It took a bite. There was a loud noise and a cloud of white smoke came out of the can.

"Go!" shouted Sarah, and the men ran to the Jeep.

Sarah and Kelly ran to the motorbike.

"Oh, no," Kelly said. One of the animals was lying across the bike. She looked at Sarah and said, "We have to do it."

The *raptor* was heavy. It seemed lifeless, but its heart was going. Its eye was open but unmoving. They lifted the animal and pulled the bike away. Then the eye moved.

"Let's go," Harding said, climbing on the bike.

◆

In the factory they put Malcolm on a table and found some food for Arby. There was no sign of the *raptors*.

"How long before the helicopter comes?" Harding asked.

"Two hours," Thorne said. "As soon as it gets light."

The time passed slowly. Levine told Malcolm about the *apatosaur* bones in the *raptors'* nest.

"The *raptors* couldn't kill so many," Malcolm said.

"Maybe they died of some sickness," Levine said.

"Yes," Malcolm said. "But they're too heavy for the *raptors* to pull to the nest. Was the nest by the river?"

"Yes," Levine said.

"Then that's it," Malcolm said. "When the *apatosaurs* die, the river carries their bodies to the nest. Food comes to the *raptors*. That's why there are so many of them, Sarah."

"But what's killing the *apatosaurs*?" Levine asked.

"Sheep, I think," Malcolm said. "When InGen first made baby dinosaurs they fed them on milk. Then they used a food made from sheep – a food that we know can cause sickness."

52

"They don't eat that food in the forest," Thorne said.

"No," Malcolm said. "But the *compys* eat the droppings of sick animals, and spread the sickness."

Levine was shocked. "But a *compy* bit me!" he said.

"Calm down, Richard," Malcolm said. "You won't die."

◆

Just before daylight, the dinosaurs came out of the trees and went straight to the Jeep. There were six of them.

"*Maiasaurs*," Levine said. "What are they doing?"

The enormous animals moved around the Jeep and began to break it up. One pulled at the soft top, another pushed the Jeep from side to side. It fell over. Something fell out.

"I don't understand it," Levine said. "These animals are not meat-eaters. They're usually peaceful."

One of the *maiasaurs* put a heavy foot on the Jeep. The others moved excitedly around something on the ground. It was a plastic box. They tried to open it with their mouths.

"Something to eat?" Levine said. "What?"

The box broke, and inside it they saw an egg. Broken. With something moving inside. There was a small sound.

"I don't believe it," Levine said, as a baby came out.

Slowly, one of the *maiasaurs* put its head down and lifted the baby up in its mouth. The others closed around it for a moment, then they all went away.

"So they came for Dodgson's egg," Malcolm said.

"And they left us without a car," Thorne said.

◆

In the first light, Dodgson's eyes opened. He was cold and his head hurt, but he was alive. Something was touching him. Small animals like chickens. Biting him. He sat up and looked

53

closer. *Compys*! Trying to eat him! They thought he was dead! He kicked them away and slowly climbed to the road. The Jeep was gone. He needed water. He began to walk.

♦

Sarah took the motorcycle back up the road to the Explorer.

"Maybe the motor's dry now," she said to Thorne. "I'll go and look at it. Use the radio to tell me what to do."

When she found the Explorer, Thorne said, "Get underneath and I'll tell you what to check."

She didn't see Dodgson coming slowly up the road. She didn't know he was there until she saw two muddy boots.

"A car!" he said, with a laugh. "Just what I need."

As he began to climb into the car she reached out with her arms and pulled his feet hard. He fell to the ground beside her. "You!" he said. "I thought you were dead!"

Harding went red with anger and moved away. Dodgson stood up. And then they felt the ground shake.

Harding turned in the mud and looked behind her. Coming up the road toward them was a *tyrannosaurus*. Quickly, Dodgson climbed under the car too. His eyes were wide with fear. Big dinosaur feet came up to the car and stopped. A head came down. The *tyrannosaur* could smell them.

At her side, Dodgson was shaking with fear. Harding was strangely calm. She knew what she had to do. Quickly, she moved her body so she could push Dodgson with her feet.

"What are you doing?" Dodgson said, in a high, frightened voice. Harding said nothing, but continued to push.

"Are you crazy?" Dodgson said. "Stop it!"

Slowly Dodgson was pushed out on to the road. The *tyrannosaur* smelled him carefully, then suddenly he was gone, his body high up in the animal's mouth. As the *tyrannosaur* turned and walked back down the road, Dodgson began to scream.

When everything was silent, Harding got back in the car and tried the motor. It started. "I'm coming back," she said into the radio.

◆

Lewis Dodgson fell. Dropped from the mouth of the *tyrannosaur* he fell through the air and landed on top of dry mud. Then he heard small noises. He looked around him. He was in the nest.

Three excited babies were looking at him. One had something around its leg. Above them, the parent watched. Dodgson stood up and turned to run. Immediately, the big adult brought his head down, knocking Dodgson over. Then the *tyrannosaur* lifted its head again and waited. Watching.

What's going on? Dodgson thought. He tried to stand up again. And again, he was knocked down. The babies came closer. Dodgson tried to move away but the adult took his leg in its mouth. Then it bit down hard. The bones broke.

Dodgson screamed in pain. He could no longer move. The babies came forward. First they took quick bites. Then, when Dodgson didn't move away, they climbed on him and began to learn how to kill.

◆

At last they were leaving the island. Everyone watched silently as it got smaller and smaller in the distance. Thorne pulled the kids to his side. "No more theories," he said. "Look at the sea. Look at the sun. Life is real. It's good to be alive. And it's *great* to be going home."

ACTIVITIES

Chapters 1–3

Before you read

1 Look at the pictures on page 2. Which of the dinosaurs are the most dangerous, do you think? Why?

2 Find these words in your dictionary.

   cage   cell   chaos   expedition   extinct   system   theory

   Which of them go in the following spaces?

   a a blood ....   **d** a medical ....   **g** a computer ....

   b a six-month ....   **e** animals ....

   c a metal ....   **f** a state of ....

3 Find these words in your dictionary:

   dinosaur   genetics   lizard   mammal

   meteorite   species   trailer

   Which of them

   a could be a plant?   **d** doesn't exist now?   **g** has wheels?

   b falls from the sky? **e** is the study of cells?

   c could be a cat?   **f** can climb walls?

After you read

4 Choose the correct answer.

   a In the 1980s, people thought dinosaurs died out because

       (i) of the Ice Age.

       (ii) they changed their behaviour.

       (iii) of a meteorite.

   b Richard Levine

       (i) doesn't believe Dr Malcolm's theory.

       (ii) thinks dinosaurs might still exist.

       (iii) thinks all dinosaurs became extinct at the same time.

   c InGen

       (i) makes scientific equipment.

       (ii) doesn't exist any more.

       (iii) owns the island of Sorna.

5 Make correct sentences.

   a Ian Malcolm   looks for dinosaurs in Costa Rica.

b	Sarah Harding	was badly hurt while he was working for InGen.
c	Richard Levine	is an engineer.
d	Lewis Dodgson	has an 11-yar-old friend.
e	Ed James	makes lots of money for Biosyn.
f	Kelly Curtis	is a spy for Biosyn.
g	Doc Thorne	studies African animals.

6 You are Richard Levine. Write down *five* things that you have brought to the island in your bag. Now compare your list with another student's. Choose the *five* most important things from both lists, and say why.

Chapters 4–6

Before you read

7 Find these words in your dictionary:
cave   helicopter   nest   volcano
Where might you find
a young birds? **b** fire and smoke? **c** big animals? **d** a pilot?

8 Why didn't Levine say where he was going, do you think? Do you think he will be found alive? Why, or why not?

After you read

9 Finish these sentences:
a Dr Malcolm knows which island Site B is on because …
b Dodgson knows where Site B is because …
c Dodgson wants to find dinosaurs because …
d Arby and Kelly get onto the island by …

10 Who or what do these words describe?
a bad smell
b good with computers
c good parents
d pink-faced and unpleasant
e too busy to help
f long neck and weak eyes
g old-fashioned
h green-brown with red lines, and tried to kill Levine

11 Malcolm says: "This island is John Hammon's dirty secret." (page 29) What does he mean?

Chapters 7–9

Before you read

12 At the end of Chapter 6, Levine says: "We've got a lot to do." What does he mean, do you think?

After you read

13 Which of these sentences are true? Correct the false ones.

  a Dodgson tries to kill Sarah Harding.

  b Raptors are afraid of parasaurs.

  c Thorne saves Sarah and Malcolm from dinosaurs.

  d Levine can't open the cage because Eddie has the key.

  e Raptors kill apatosaurs and carry them to their nest.

  f Tyrannosaurs kill three people.

14 What do you think will happen to the dinosaurs on the island at the end of the story?

Writing

15 You are Kelly or Arby. Your teacher asks you to write about your summer vacation. What will you write?

16 Choose *two* of the following, and say how they are important to the story.

  a computers **b** Sarah Harding **c** tyrannosaurs

17 Choose *two* of the dinosaurs on Isla Sorna and write a detailed description of them. Describe their appearance and behavior. What do you find most interesting or surprising about them?

18 You are Ian Malcolm. You want to make another expedition to Isla Sorna. Write a report about your last visit. What mistakes did you make? What will you do to make your next expedition less dangerous?

Answers for the activities in this book are published in our free resource packs for teachers, the Penguin Readers Factsheets, or available on a separate sheet. Please write to your local Pearson Education office or to: Marketing Department, Penguin Longman Publishing, 5 Bentinck Street, London W1M 5RN.